ANIMUS

SLEEPING DRAGONS BOOK 1

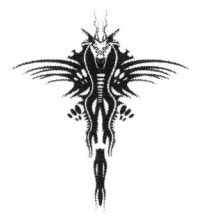

OPHELIA BELL

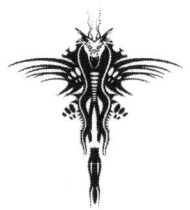

Animus
Copyright © 2014 Ophelia Bell
Cover Art Designed by Dawné Dominique
Photograph Copyrights © Fotolio.com, DepositPhotos.com, CanStock.com

All rights reserved. No part of this book may be reproduced in any form or by any electronic means, including information storage and retrieval systems, without permission in writing from the author, except by a reviewer who may quote brief passages in review.

This is a work of fiction. Names, places, characters, and events are fictitious in every regard. Any similarities to actual events and persons, living or dead, is purely coincidental. Any trademarks, service marks, product names, or named features are assumed to be the property of their respective owners, and are used only for reference. There is no implied endorsement if any of these terms are used.

Published by Ophelia Bell
UNITED STATES

ISBN-13: 978-1544268859
ISBN-10: 1544268858

Also by Ophelia Bell

Sleeping Dragons Series

Animus
Tabula Rasa
Gemini
Shadows
Nexus
Ascend

Rising Dragons Series

Night Fire
Breath of Destiny
Breath of Memory
Breath of Innocence
Breath of Desire
Breath of Love
Breath of Flame & Shadow
Breath of Fate
Sisters of Flame

Immortal Dragons Series

Dragon Betrayed
Dragon Blues
Dragon Void
Dragon Splendor
Dragon Rebel

Standalone Erotic Tales

After You
Out of the Cold

Ophelia Bell Taboo

Burying His Desires

•

Blackmailing Benjamin
Betraying Benjamin
Belonging to Benjamin

•

Casey's Secrets
Casey's Discovery
Casey's Surrender

What can awaken a sleeping dragon?

Preface

What is an Animus?

The short answer? An "animus" is that sex-loving beast that lives inside every woman. If this book sparked your interest, you know what I'm talking about.

In Jungian psychology, the "animus" refers to the male aspect of the female psyche, just as the "anima" is the converse in men. Using this concept as the launching point for my series, my goal was to personify the animus aspect in particular. Therefore we get dragons, which are my interpretation of the animus as the female "lizard brain" and the root of a woman's sexuality.

It's purely unscientific, of course, and the Jungian archetypes are only loosely represented in the series, but the animus aspect (my interpretation thereof, at any rate) is the strongest and continues throughout all the dragon books, particularly in the strength, independence, and unapologetically sexual nature of my female characters, even the ones who are just discovering their sexuality.

Embrace your inner dragon!

—Ophelia Bell

CHAPTER ONE

Erika always got a little damp between the thighs when on the cusp of an archaeological find, but this wasn't just any old pile of ancient bones she was about to uncover. Today her entire body thrummed with excitement. If her coordinates were right, this would be the find of the century.

The vine-covered rock wall in front of her was the final barrier. Her heart pounded in anticipation of what she hoped lay beneath. With passionate rips, she yanked the foliage away to display the elaborate, smooth carving of a dragon wound into the shape of a disc.

The image sent a thrill through her. *Hot damn, we found it!* The culmination of her hard years of graduate research rested in the darkness somewhere behind that slab of vine-covered rock. She and her team would be the first to set eyes on it.

In spite of her conviction that they'd finally reached the end of their quest, she glanced back to her geologist for confirmation, itching with impatience.

Eben's eyes widened and he looked up from the handheld GPS unit. "I just sprung wood, baby," he said, echoing her own thoughts. "Fuck yeah! This is it!"

Cheers erupted from the group behind them. They deserved to celebrate after enduring an exhausting trek through the remote reaches of the Sumatran jungle to get here, but the true celebration would have to wait just a little bit longer.

"Yeah, but it's just a wall." Erika swept her hands over the ridged face of the stone slab in front of her, ripping down more vines as she went. "How do we get inside, assuming there's an inside to get to?"

Eben slunk up behind her, pressing his tall, muscular body against her back. His hands covered hers while they explored the rock face. The scent of his heady musk hit her nose, and then much lower regions, when she inhaled.

"Maybe extra hands are necessary," he whispered in her ear. "Those old dwarves could be horny bastards, wanting their stones touched by everyone."

"Dwarves ... You've been watching too many movies. But I know *someone's* a horny bastard," she whispered, shifting her backside away from his obvious hard-on. He didn't seem to notice, moving around her to inspect the wall more closely.

She let him take over their exploration of the hard surface before them. Eben had an uncanny ability to suss out the secrets of just about any mineral. He also had a particular skill at sinking his rock-hard shaft into her deeper crevices whenever the mood struck them. It was why she'd been so attracted to him during their undergrad years. Post-graduation, she'd kept him around because he was every bit as ambitious as she was to explore the deeper reaches of the world and all their secrets. It also didn't hurt that the tall, irreverent blond was very easy on the eyes.

But their relationship had shifted since the start of this expedition. Her desire for Eben was rooted purely in necessity. He had always been more than happy to scratch her near-constant itch, but his remedy to her overactive libido was gradually growing less and less effective.

Erika's drive to find this temple was ever-present during her waking hours, overtaking even that craving for sex. When she slept, it was a different story. The need to successfully complete an expedition and bring back proof she could rub in all her colleagues' faces was just the surface of what pushed her on.

The source of her itch — the strange dreams she'd endured since she was a teen — had grown more detailed the deeper she dug into the existence of dragons. Now the dreams haunted her nightly with images of a beautiful, virile, red-haired man. One whose voice still echoed in her mind during daylight hours, who promised her the kind of partner she'd had yet to find among even the most adventurous of her fearless friends and acquaintances.

She'd once been convinced it would take an older man to truly satisfy her, but the closer she got to proving dragons existed, the more Erika wondered if what she needed wasn't even a man at all.

"Here," Eben said, pushing her fingertips into a cleft she hadn't noticed. She grabbed onto the edge of the fissure and followed it down, pressing until she felt it give. She gasped when the entire face in front of them receded at least a foot and shifted aside with the rough grinding of stone on stone. More cheers sounded behind them as their team looked on.

"We're inside!" she yelled, pulling away from Eben and raising her arms up in triumph.

Cool, dry air rushed out, carrying with it a familiar, pungent aroma. Her skin prickled with gooseflesh at the memories that surfaced in response to that scent as much as from the sudden chill of the air.

She'd been dreaming of this place ever since her dad had hinted at a mythical dragon race, spinning bedtime stories that rivaled those her friends had heard from their parents when they were children. Her more sexual dreams didn't begin until she was older, but they were no less tied to that seed of curiosity she'd cultivated since girlhood.

In retrospect, she believed her father had left his research notes out deliberately to entice her. She'd read them over multiple times from age ten onward, and had fantasized ever since about finding the elusive dragon temple her father had been searching for. All he'd had were small clues, one of which was the tiny jade carving of a dragon she wore around her neck. Another was a jade bottle, empty, yet still holding the lingering, spicy scent of whatever substance it had once contained.

Her father had died wondering, and Erika had vowed that she would continue his search.

The dreams began around the time she graduated from high school, shortly after she lost her virginity and discovered the wondrous pleasure sex could bring. It was like her first real orgasm had flipped a switch in her mind, signaling that her deep subconscious was fair game for some mysterious, otherworldly dream creature to play in.

* * *

The dreams always began with the scent of spice, a distinctly male aroma that enveloped her before the images themselves solidified. He appeared then, leaning against a tree in a misty garden beside a brick path.

She thought it might be one of the paths that led between the buildings of the university where she'd tagged along with her father for work as a child, and then eventually attended herself after high school. But this man who greeted her looked nothing like any of the male students she'd ever encountered.

"I missed you, Erika," he said, standing up and stalking toward her with that intense red stare of his. He wore a loose-fitting linen shirt and breeches that looked to be from another era. "When are you coming for me?"

She smirked and tilted her head. "As soon as you make me."

He laughed and shook his head. "You are a wicked girl. I will make you come soon enough, but you know what I mean. I'm going out of my mind waiting for you. You and all those delicious orgasms I plan to give you once we're together in the flesh."

"My life is about more than sex, you know. I have a lot of work left before I can find you. Now that I know where you are, I need a team who I trust. I'm making a list, but I'm missing one more member. Once I find the last person, you bet your ass I'm coming."

"Good," he said, lifting his hand and cupping the back of her head. She tilted back to gaze up into his handsome face and those fathomless eyes that beheld her like two smoldering embers. Her core heated as his exotic scent grew thicker, the fog around her turning red as he bent and covered her mouth with his.

"Sweet Mother, I wish you were real," he murmured as he laid Erika down on the damp grass, unbuttoning her shirt as they went and baring her breasts to the cool air.

He worshipped her nipples with his tongue and she savored the pleasure, ignoring that dull ache in her chest at his reminder that this was all just a dream. When he moved up to kiss her, she moaned into his mouth and gripped his shoulders, overcome with unexpected urgency.

She twisted beneath him, slinging one leg around his hip and flipping them both until she straddled his waist. Glaring down at him, she said, "You are real, and so am I. And I will fucking find you, I promise."

His gaze burned as he pulled desperately at her waistband. "What if this is just a dream? I want it to be real, but nothing real has ever felt this good, this ... fundamental. I've never wanted a woman as much as I want you. Never needed one."

Erika lifted her hips, shifting her legs enough for him to push her pants down so she could shuck them off. She kept her gaze fixed on his as she tore open his breeches and freed his cock, then wasted no time sinking down onto the gloriously thick, hard shaft.

"Oh, god, I need you, too. I've never needed a man before. They're intimidated by me, only worth my time if they're good for a fuck or willing to entertain my crazy research. You ... sweet fucking Jesus, you're everything I want."

ANIMUS

"Why, Erika?" he said, his fingertips sinking deep to her hips as he thrust up into her, the slick friction driving her wild and making that confounding ache in her chest turn to pure, molten fire.

"Because you are my research. You are a dragon. You are everything I'm working for. So you have to exist. You can't be just a dream. Oh, god, please don't be just a dream."

She threw back her head and cried out, her last plea to him repeated into the foggy ether surrounding them as she climaxed. His thrusts quickened and deepened, and a second later, he roared her name in just the way he always did in these dreams.

When she collapsed against him, clinging desperately to the last remnants of the dream, he whispered the same thing as always into her ear: "You are mine, sweet Erika. Come for me, even if it is only in my dreams."

* * *

Would those dreams come true today? She had come for him as she'd promised, was about to cross the threshold with that same spicy fragrance brimming in her lungs with each breath. All she could think about as that aroma inundated her was how her dream lover smelled when his hot body was wrapped around her, his cock buried deep inside, and his low voice rumbling in her ear, *"Mine."*

Erika shivered at the memory, her nipples hardening. At least she could pass the reaction off as a response to the temperature of the air inside the chamber and not her arousal at the memories those scents drew from her mind.

CHAPTER TWO

The opening displayed a dark corridor lined with smooth, pale stone. Erika reached inside and slid her fingertips across the rock. In spite of the cooler air beyond the threshold, the warmth of the walls sank into her fingertips. Once the door stopped sliding open with a heavy *ka-chunk*, a series of recessed sconces that lined the corridor began to glow one by one.

"Whoa," Eben said. "Magic?"

"Engineering, most likely. Old school ... I bet there's a trigger somewhere in that door pocket that lights these up when the door is opened. Hey, Corey!" she called back behind them. "You'll love these lights. Get up here and document how they work."

The athletic, dark-haired tech nodded from behind his digital camera. "You got it, boss."

Erika held her eagerness at bay for the time being. Instead of giving in to the urge to run inside and explore, she took over camera duty for Corey and let him do his job. He diligently tested the air quality and gave her a swift thumbs-up, indicating all was good on that front. The glowing sconces, on the other hand, made his dark eyebrows arch high on his tanned brow.

"It's like nothing I've ever seen," he said. "They come pretty close to light bulbs, but we both know better than that. Take a look ..." He reached a leather-gloved hand into one of the half-moon-shaped recesses. What he pulled out continued to glow when he held it up before her.

Heat radiated off the oblong shape. It was round and bulbous at the lit end, dark and tapered at the end Corey held. The other members of Erika's team circled around, murmuring in awe while the glow gradually subsided. When it emitted only the brightness of a low-burning ember, Erika reached out a tentative finger to touch it. Heat still lingered in it, but it felt solid, more like a stone than a fragile glass bulb.

"See?" Eben said. "*Magic.*"

She rolled her eyes and took the odd stone from Corey, her first artifact from the temple. Corey grinned at what she was sure had to be a giddy expression on her face. She certainly felt like a kid on Christmas morning.

"Ready to conquer the dragon temple?" Corey asked with a quirk of his mouth and a wink. The epitome of professional behavior and honorable to a fault, Corey had always felt like the protective older brother of the group. Erika eyed him curiously now. Even though he'd traveled with three very attractive, intelligent—and single—women for months, he tended toward broody and solitary. Not once had he given any hint of flirting, until now.

Dismissing his odd behavior as a side effect of the same excitement that afflicted her entire team, she returned his camera to him, turned back to the doorway, and with a deep breath, stepped into the opening, caressing the pale stone walls as she went. The lights illuminated the translucent stone at a warm simmer, and she could just make out the beginning of a staircase several yards ahead.

"Jesus, this place is paneled entirely in jade." She paused to study a section of the wall, noting the faint green and gold coloring that threaded through the white stone in amorphous serpentine patterns. Once she reached the end of the corridor, she paused to stare down at a staircase plunging farther than she could see.

"Are you down there?" she whispered into the darkness, her spine tingling in anticipation of what she would find — *who* she would find below. Every molecule in her being told Erika her dream lover would be there, even though the logical part of her brain still screamed that it made no scientific sense for her to believe it. Still, she wasn't one to turn her back on a challenge like this. She would trust the evidence — whatever it happened to be.

"You guys ready for this?" she asked the group behind her.

Of course they were ready, she chided herself. But was *she* ready? So far the place had exceeded her wildest dreams, and she was barely in the door. How deep would it go? What kinds of wonders would she find? And the biggest question that occupied her mind: Would she be able to prove all her father's research true? If there really were dragons down there — if *he* was down there — would he be as intelligent and powerful as her father's notes suggested?

Too many questions, but she was a scientist. The only thing to do was ... Well, fuck. *Boldly go, dammit! That's what you do!*

As if sensing her hesitance, Eben stepped up beside Erika and placed his hand on her shoulder. "Need someone to hold onto, babe? This is your discovery. You should be the one to take the first step down. We're all right behind you."

After the first step, her anxiety disappeared and her excitement returned. It took a lot of effort to maintain a casual pace, curiosity making her itch to move faster. A hundred feet into the depths, she began taking steps two at a time, impatient to get to the good part. How deep was this place?

Fifteen minutes later, they finally reached the bottom and were faced with an elaborately decorated door. Onyx and gold gleamed in the light coming from a pair of larger sconces that flanked the door. Its decorations depicted several dragons who appeared to be tangled in the throes of mating, but not with other dragons. All their partners appeared human. In the center of the carved coil of bodies was a small, circular depression with a starburst pattern of upraised black nubs.

"What kind of crazy sex dungeon did you bring us to, Erika?" Dimitri asked, his words accented with subtle drawn-out syllables that belied his Greek ancestry. He stifled a chuckle. "Not that I'd complain, but that looks kinky even for me."

Erika sighed. "Y'know, Dimitri, sometimes I wonder if I didn't pick *the* horniest team on the planet. But maybe you guys are meant to be here. All the lore I've managed to find suggests that dragons have particular sexual appetites. And I suppose this is our first clue that it was accurate."

They paused to take pictures and record more for the ongoing documentary they'd been filming. The door was locked, but they were prepared for this one. Eben pulled out the solid gold disk they'd found a month ago in Myanmar and fitted it into the depression. It seated perfectly, the nubs in the door filling inside the small holes within the disk. Eben twisted it and the door swung open, almost seeming to float on invisible hinges.

"I've got another hard-on," Eben whispered in her ear. She elbowed him and he laughed, but she had to admit she was aroused by the way that scent kept teasing at her senses, bringing to mind all the glorious dream images she'd had over the years of red eyes and a tongue that could do wickedly naughty things to her body.

Beyond the door, they all paused. Her entire team let out a combined exhalation of awe.

The chamber beyond was immense, with long, curved walls, white and illuminated with recessed lights like the corridor they'd just passed through. The entry led down another staircase to the center of an amphitheater surrounded by tiers of stone benches extending all the way back to the far walls. At the opposite end from the entry was a high dais occupied by a throne elaborately carved out of jade, its translucent hue reflecting the light cast from behind it.

"Wow, check those out," Eben said. "Nothing like what we'd imagined they might be."

He pointed toward the pair of massive white dragon guardians that flanked the throne, and Erika's eyes widened at the sight. The guardians each rested on their haunches, supported from behind by thick tails. Both sported huge, erect phalluses jutting up from between their scaled thighs. They'd have made interesting guest seats, that was for certain.

"Yeah," Erika said. "That's almost obscene, isn't it?"

He chuckled. "No more than you shoving my face into your wet pussy and telling me to eat you like a starving man ..."

She dug a knuckle into his ribs and glanced around to see who might have heard, but the others were already spread out, scouting the room. Not that it was any secret that she and Eben occasionally slept together. That kind of thing was hard to keep quiet when you shared a campsite with five other people for weeks at a stretch. But she knew Camille had a thing for Eben and didn't want to rub the younger woman's face in it. Erika's relationship with Eben had always been built out of convenience and mutual need. She'd long ago sensed he had a limit that he would hit before she hit her own. He'd been her best friend for years, but he wasn't the man she was meant to be with any more than she was the woman for him.

The image of those lust-filled red eyes returned to her mind, along with the deep, resonating voice and the touch laying claim to her body. *"Mine."* She shivered with an unexpected wave of arousal and looked around, wondering where her dream lover might be if he were indeed in here somewhere. He had to be, the way her body was suddenly lit up.

"Look at those doorways behind the dais." She pointed at the pair of double-doors that rested deep on either side of the throne. "What do you think is back there?"

Eben shrugged. "The dungeon? The kitchen? What do dragons eat anyway? Pretty virgin princesses?" He glanced at Camille, who was still gaping in awe in the doorway just out of earshot of his joke. "If I were a dragon I'd *love* eating virgins."

Eben grinned at Erika, irritatingly confident that she'd appreciate his sense of humor. He walked down the stairs and crossed the floor in long strides, taking the steps up to the throne two at a time with her following close behind.

"I wonder why the throne is empty," he said. "Usually an elaborate religious display like this would have the object of worship in plain sight."

Erika countered sharply. "You're a geologist. What the hell do you know about religious displays? To me, this looks like a place to hold court. Not symbolic. Functional. See the alcoves in the mezzanine?" She pointed at the second tier above them. "I'd bet you anything those lead to more rooms, maybe back into the surrounding structure as well. This place is more than just a shrine, it's a compound. People—or dragons—actually lived here." *And maybe they still do.*

"Well, I guess we'll have to wait for the experts to say otherwise, huh?" He raised an eyebrow and crouched in front of one of the draconic figures flanking the throne. "They look so real, like they could wake up at any second."

"Master artisans, I guess." She walked up to the other statue and stroked the dragon's snout affectionately, trailing her fingertips over its polished white brows and the curling horns extending backward from its skull. Her fingertips tingled strangely and her nipples hardened against her coarse linen shirt. The texture of the stone sparked memories of her dreams—of the feel of hard, scaled flesh beneath her palms and the huge, red-skinned half-man, half-beast who possessed her body through the night. She had to find him.

The stone was so smooth and warm it would have felt like flesh, if it had any give to it. It was polished to leave no evidence of the maker's tools anywhere. When she looked over at Eben, he was stroking the prominent stone phallus of the dragon statue in front of him, the lewd gesture instantly clearing her mind of the delicious fantasy she'd been having.

"I can't take you anywhere," she said.

"Tell me you don't want to play with it. They're all so ... anatomically correct. I always wondered what a dragon's dick looked like. Almost as nice as mine. And it's so *smooth*. Seriously, you need to touch it."

"It's just a reflection of their virility." Her heartbeat sped up. Her assessment was accurate from an academic standpoint, but the growing heat between her thighs made her sure there had to be more to these statues than met the eye.

"So erect cocks are only symbolic, is that what you're saying?"

Erika gave him a sidelong glance. "In a statue, yeah. In you, it just means you haven't jerked off in a few hours." She looked pointedly at the huge bulge in his crotch.

"I always have a cock. It's not my fault if you're too big a prude to want to touch it," he muttered.

She scowled at him, knowing he was digging at her for kicking him out of her tent the night before, but she'd been too distracted by their imminent discovery to entertain him. Her plan had been to find that semi-dream state where her fantasy lover existed, imagine the things he did to her in her dreams, and rub out enough orgasms to send herself into a mini-coma so she could sleep through the night without the distraction of another body beside her.

It was unlike Eben to take issue with a night apart, but her sexual interest in him had waned the moment they'd set foot in this jungle. She'd probably taken advantage of his eagerness to please her one time too many. He'd just as soon go hungry when they were in a tiff, rather than come begging to her for sustenance of the carnal variety.

A hesitant throat cleared nearby and they both glanced up. Camille stood fidgeting, her bright blue eyes locked onto Eben's hand where it still absently stroked the rod of polished stone.

"What is it, Cammy?" Erika asked.

"Uh ... um ... Do you mind if I start translating?" Camille asked, darting a look at Erika. "Everything is covered with text. Well, almost everything." Camille's attention slid back to Eben's hand on the dragon statue's cock. Erika narrowed her eyes when she caught the wicked smile on Eben's face while he watched Camille blush.

"Have at it," Erika said. "The sooner we find out the secrets of this place, the better, right? The boys can set up camp. It's their night, anyway."

Camille nodded and left, clutching and twisting at the end of her long, blonde braid, a nervous habit she only seemed to affect when she was around Eben.

"You're such an asshole sometimes," Erika said. "She's got the hots for you and you keep taunting her like that. It's not fair."

He chuckled and let go of the dragon's penis. "I'd love a taste of her, but I have a feeling she's nowhere near as experienced as you. I like women who take the initiative."

"Or men?" she asked, reminded of his excuse after she'd found him entangled with a fellow geology TA named Jared. Eben had been cocky enough to invite her to join them, but she'd been too shocked to take advantage of the opportunity. Later when she questioned him about it, all he'd said was, "He asked."

Eben shrugged. "Depends on the man, but yeah." His expression grew thoughtful as he turned to watch Camille bend over to extract a notebook from her gear. "I don't know ... maybe I could teach her something."

Erika let out a long-suffering sigh. "Behave yourself while we're here, all right? I can't have my linguist falling to pieces mid-month because you popped her cherry and she's too in love to keep working."

"Yes, mistress," he said with a gleam in his eye.

Chapter Three

Geva mentally strained at his bonds for the hundredth time in the last few hours. The temple where he and the rest of the dragon brood slept had finally been discovered after five centuries of waiting. His hibernation was due to end, and he couldn't wait to be free.

Yet again, he imagined the first thing he would do once he was liberated from this prison and able to fly above the human world. He would seek out one of the nearby villages and use the seductive powers of his smoky breath to incite another orgy. Then he would bask in the debauchery, soaking up all the delicious sexual energy there was to be had. After that, maybe he would get back to the business of behaving and perform whatever duties were required of him by his queen. Just not until he'd had his fill of beautiful, nubile young women and men. His cock throbbed at the very thought.

"You'll do no such thing."

Inwardly, Geva cursed. It seemed his keeper had been roused by the breach of their temple as well.

"Why shouldn't I? You want it as much as I do, Issa. It can't have been comfortable having to sit like a Guardian all this time,

just to make sure my bonds were secure before the other Court dragons took their places."

He lay prone on a huge stone slab, entirely petrified in red jade. As if it weren't enough that the hibernation ritual turned them all into stone, the old Guardians who prepared the temple had also bound him in chains. And all because he'd broken the rules the week before his hibernation began.

Being the son of the reigning dragon queen hadn't helped his case one bit. He'd risked being discovered for what he was, but there had been no *real* danger of that. All the humans in that town had enjoyed letting loose and fucking to their hearts' content. Geva had immensely enjoyed it himself, and had taken a taste of just about all the humans involved during the couple days it had gone on, up until he'd been discovered and hauled away for the hibernation ritual that was about to begin.

At least he'd gone out with a bang.

Issa's voice rang through his mind again, reminding him of the thing he'd rather forget. *"You will have a mate once the ritual to awaken us is complete. One of those humans out there belongs to you. I know you have dreamed of her recently. I hear you utter her name sometimes while you slumber."*

"She's nothing more than a means to an end," Geva snarled back. *"Hers is merely the sweet cunt that will melt this prison when she slides down my cock and gives me her Nirvana for the first time. She'll be but one of many treasures I intend to collect once I rejoin the world and can claim my birthright. I'll be as wealthy as Gavra, the first Red, was, with hundreds of pets at my disposal. I won't stop fucking for the next five centuries."*

Somehow he could almost sense Issa's eyes rolling. She was his closest friend, and though she hadn't actually condoned the antics that had gotten him chained up in his hibernation chamber with her as his guardian, she'd definitely been tempted. Female blue dragons were like that—always teetering on the razor's edge between lust and propriety. The more red that tinged their scales, the more they leaned toward lust. Issa was a deep shade of lavender, so he knew how difficult it must have been for her to resist the lure of all the orgasmic power flying around that day.

"Our ways have been changing, Geva. Every generation the Court takes fewer mates. Your mother only had your father, remember? And my parents were exclusive to each other, too. A deeper bond with fewer mates means we get to keep them for longer."

The prospect of five centuries in a new world was daunting enough without being forced to think of how he'd fare with only a single mate. No ... he preferred to imagine hundreds of women who eagerly invited his touch, who begged for his cock or his tongue. Not his heart.

The problem was that over the last couple decades, all those women he liked to fantasize about had begun to have the same pretty face, the same dark, silken hair ... the same luscious backside and throaty cries when he fucked her.

Them. When he fucked *them.* Not one woman. One woman wasn't enough for a Red as powerful as he was.

Soft laughter teased at his mind.

"What do you find so funny?" he groused.

"That you deny her so vehemently whenever she crosses your mind. I can picture her face as clearly as you do now, after being stuck in this chamber with you for so long. She is a lovely one, and judging from the spark she has, more than enough for a male like you. What was her name again? It was a familiar one ..."

"Don't say it, Issa."

"It started with an 'E' ..."

"Issa ..." he warned, not wanting her to put voice to the syllables which had haunted him so often as of late, which evoked such vibrant images of the female who, at this moment, was so close by he could almost scent her through the chamber's heavy stone door.

"Erika."

He groaned, his mind suddenly awash in images of the female herself, of all the dreams he'd had of her eagerly indulging his myriad erotic whims. If his every fantasy could be embodied in a single human female, it would be this female. She was far too perfect to actually exist, though.

"*There's no way she's real.*"

"*If she isn't real, then neither is the male I've been dreaming of, and I really would rather believe he is.*"

Chapter Four

After exploring for a time, Erika and her team erected their equipment and set up camp in one of the four alcoves that flanked the mezzanine. Each of the alcoves possessed a fire pit that seemed to work the same way the wall sconces had and put out sufficient heat for cooking. They settled into camp to plan their study and catalog their finds.

Kris began cooking dinner. Within moments, the entire area was awash in aromatic spices that made Erika's mouth water and distracted her from her planning. She'd only mapped out a fraction of the compound that afternoon. They had mostly encountered a lot of jade corridors lined with locked doors. Tomorrow she would focus on the doors, but now she was distracted by a deeper need. It was like an itch she couldn't scratch—a presence in her mind filled with a deep craving she couldn't explain. She shoved it aside for the time being to eat dinner, thanking Kris when he brought a steaming bowl of curry and rice to her.

The sculpted Thai made Erika think of a Mongolian warrior sometimes. While she ate the spicy food, she imagined him naked on horseback, clad only in scant fur armor, coming to ravage her. The delicate flavors of her dinner made her salivate more with every bite; the spice on her tongue sent a zing of pleasure straight between her thighs. Her nipples pricked and a sheen of sweat broke out on her skin. She found it tough to keep her eyes off Kris now, or any of the men, for that matter. Yet when she looked at each one, she saw something more, as though they each embodied the essence of that strange man from her dreams.

She shook her head, trying to dispel the fantasy, and took a deep breath. These men worked for her. Aside from Eben, she'd never have entertained a tryst with any of them as long as they had a professional relationship, but that didn't mean she couldn't appreciate what she saw.

They were all attractive, though Eben had always been the most forward one of the group. Dimitri was soft-spoken, though quick-witted, and flirted in a very subdued manner with everyone, even the other men. His sweet face and short-cropped blond hair afforded him a resemblance to a Nordic god. His full lips mesmerized her for a moment as she watched him consume the delicious food. Her heart sped up when his tongue darted out to lick his lips. She shifted her gaze away, replying to the group's steady banter mindlessly while her eyes continued to roam.

Corey ate quickly in general, but tonight he seemed to savor the meal for a change. He took slow bites in between conversation about their find. The normally prominent lines beside his blue eyes relaxed, making him look ten years younger, and oh what a pretty boy he must have been when he was in his mid-to-late twenties like the rest of them. Now he was a very attractive man who'd probably been hurt one time too many, if the sad look in his eyes was any indication. He'd always been the most aloof member of the group, but he'd been a more than competent team member during their arduous trek to get here.

Camille was still giving Eben that puppy-dog look, but appeared more flushed this time, her glance periodically darting to his crotch. Erika eyed Eben's lap and raised an eyebrow. The man still had a hard-on. What the hell was up with him? He'd been a tad oversexed for at least as long as they'd known each other, but this was something new. She glanced around at the others to gauge their relative levels of excitement. When she met Hallie's gaze, the pretty brunette raised an eyebrow and shot a pointed look at Eben. Erika just rolled her eyes in response and smiled.

Hallie was the reliable one. Even though Erika was sure she hid some deeper darkness, Hallie wasn't afraid to share her opinion, and had eagerly and competently jumped at every task Erika assigned. She had also managed to adeptly rebuff Eben's periodic advances. Erika had wondered if the woman was gay until they'd actually talked and she expressed that she preferred men who were just a little more mysterious.

"Why not Corey?" Erika had asked.

Hallie had pursed her lips and confided, "He's way too laser-focused on his own agenda. I don't do casual sex and neither does he, from what I can gather. If I'm gonna sleep with a guy, I need to know he's doing it because he wants me—not some feminine ideal I probably wouldn't live up to anyway."

But now Hallie had pulled her long hair up and was fanning her face while she eyed Kris. Kris was the mysterious native, his Asian features a contrast to the other men. He'd spent their weeks-long trek being the ideal guide, regaling them with stories of the jungles they traveled through, protecting them from potential predators, and cooking the best food they'd ever tasted. Yet he'd shared very little about himself. Mysterious didn't begin to cover the large man who was now collecting their dishes to clean up, smiling politely at each of them as he went around the camp.

One thing she did note when he collected her bowl was the unmistakable bulge of an erection pressing against the front of his khaki shorts. It caught her eye before she could censor herself. When she looked up at him a second later, he just smiled and said, "Still hungry?"

She blinked at him and swallowed. A vivid image of taking his cock in her mouth right there blazed across her mind and her thighs clenched involuntarily. What the hell was happening to her?

"Ah ... I'm full." Full was an understatement ... she'd have loved to be full of him. So much that her vaginal muscles ached. God, she wouldn't normally think of it so clinically, but the feeling was akin to an affliction now. It was no longer just a dull itch, but a very present distraction bordering on discomfort, one only made worse by the low-pitched whisper of a male voice inside her head. It was the same one that had occupied her dreams for years, but now seemed to be bleeding into her waking hours.

"Thanks for another great dinner, Kris. I'll be right back." Erika stood and wandered into the dimly lit corridor leading to the back of the alcove behind the tiers of the amphitheater seats.

Past the offshoots of a side-corridor she knew spanned the circumference of the temple was a cozy rear chamber harboring a fountain made of the ubiquitous jade. Its water spilled into a shallow pool, and the space was lit with the same small globes that had come to life when she and her research team had opened the outer doors.

Erika bent over the edge of the pool and splashed water on her heated face, undid a few buttons of her shirt, and splashed more onto her chest. Something in the air made her too hot. It couldn't just be the excitement of finding the temple. Ever since they'd opened the doors, she'd grown more and more aroused, finding it nearly impossible to stop thinking of that man from her dreams who owned her so completely with his touch.

It wasn't unlike her to want sex after a find like this, but she normally had control over her fantasies. Here she feared she was completely losing it. She was driven to the point of insane lust and she couldn't shake the sense that she was close now. Close to *him*, whoever the hell he was. And as fearless an explorer as she tended to be, the idea of proving her dream lover was real terrified her.

She shook her head again, trying to clear it of the cobwebs of desire. She was a scientist, she had to keep a level head, remain analytical about the situation, even if her thesis *had* stated that dragons existed, which was ludicrous on a good day.

"You okay?"

The deep voice startled her. "Oh, hi, Kris. Yeah ... I think so. This place is pretty epic. I guess I'm just a bit overwhelmed by it."

"You don't look okay. Did the magic get to you already? I tried to keep the spice light tonight."

She blinked at him, not sure she'd heard right. "Magic ... what magic? And the spice was fine."

He looked around like there might be invisible things floating in the air, then smirked at her.

"Dragon magic. It's everywhere. It's affected me, too. Dragons are horny beasts."

"Not Dwarves?" she asked, shakily laughing about Eben's earlier joke.

"Nah ... Dwarves are a myth. Dragons are real, and they live here." He leaned closer and said in a conspiratorial voice, "And they feed on our pleasure."

His words made her quiver and she had to close her eyes to get herself under control. When she opened them again, Kris was kneeling beside the pool and stripping off his shirt. His shoulders rippled in the warm glow of the lights. He leaned over the edge of the pool, bracing both hands at the lip, and plunged his entire upper body through the surface, down into the cool water. She watched the expanse of his olive skin submerge, the tattoos that twined around his torso nearly obscured.

A single huge dragon adorned his body, its head draped across his back, eyeing her steadily from where it rested on the surface of one bunched shoulder. It coiled around him in a proprietary fashion, its tail twining around his waist. The eyes of the tattoo seemed to follow her.

Kris emerged from the pool and flipped his head back, flinging water behind him. He sat gasping and blinking, his glistening form covered with little rivulets of water. Erika's mouth watered, and her pussy began to tingle in a way not unlike her tongue had during dinner.

"It won't take long," he said cryptically, swiping a hand down his face and flinging water off into a corner.

"What won't take long?"

"The magic. You don't really need to translate the text for it to happen. It's your destiny as much as it is mine. Now that you're in the current of the magic, it'll take you where it needs you to be, to the dragon Fate has claimed you for."

"And where is that?" she asked, latching onto his words. Did he know where her dragon was? Wait … Why the hell was she humoring him? He was speaking nonsense. Magic? She needed to get hold of herself, for Christ's sake. As much as she wanted it all to be true, she was still a scientist, bound by logic and an analytic mind. It shouldn't be that easy to just let go of everything she'd been taught.

Kris raked fingers through his wet hair and stood up, gesturing down the shadowed corridor. "I'll show you."

"Should I be scared?" she asked, the result of the last shred of logic in her.

He chuckled and let his eyes drift down over her sweaty, dirty trekking shirt that was already half undone. The fabric was soaked through from the water she'd splashed on her chest to counteract the heat welling from deep within her. Her nipples were clearly visible, pressing against the weave.

"With tits like yours, no." Kris took a deep breath through his nose and closed his eyes, as if savoring some aroma that lingered in the air. "And power that sweet, definitely not. Your dragon will be very pleased when you awaken him."

Her dragon? "Who the hell are you?"

"Your guide." He grinned and turned to walk away.

"Wait!" Erika yelled after him, then ran to catch up. "What the fuck about the fucking dragon magic?"

"It's everywhere in here," he replied with a wave of his arm that made the muscles in his broad back flex alluringly. "And it's the strongest it's been since they were sent to sleep half a millennium ago. Now it's time for them to wake and live in the world again. To mate with the humans Fate promised them."

Chapter Five

Kris led her down a pale corridor that glowed with magic dragon light, or she supposed that's what it was now. She felt a little drugged. Her skin tingled, so sensitive the rub of the material of her shirt over her nipples sent jolts of pleasure through her with every stride. She'd been horny enough upon opening the doorway into this place, but now her normally healthy appetite seemed to be magnified tenfold. *Magic,* she thought. A little thrill went through her at the memory of some of the stories her father had told her, but she still wasn't quite prepared to believe it. The dreams, though ... was she prepared to believe *them*? Was her desire for that elusive red-eyed man strong enough for her to abandon her scientific principles?

"I guess magic *might* explain Eben's perma-boner," she joked, trying to dispel her anxiety. It might also explain the personal porn video that kept running through her mind—the one of Kris nailing her against the warm jade of the temple wall, or bending her over the edge of the pool and fucking her from behind, or countless other scenarios she'd imagined just in the span of the last fifteen minutes, not the least of which involved *him*, her dragon.

In a moment, they emerged at the back of the main room, outside one of the heavy carved doors that flanked the dais.

"Those doors are locked," she said.

Kris smiled back at her. "Not if you know how to open them." He pushed against the smooth surface of the door. It swung open just enough for them to slip into the darkness beyond. More sconces lit, illuminating a row of closed doors set deep into the curved wall of the corridor, each one set between a pair of majestic white jade dragons similar to the ones that stood guard beside the throne in the main chamber. All of them sported erections similar to the one Eben had so lewdly stroked earlier. Kris paused in front of the first door, one carved out of red and lavender jade.

"This door will kick off the ritual. Then this ..." He moved to stand in front of the door beside it, staring up at the shimmering golden carvings. Not gilt, Erika realized when she looked closely, but more carved jade in a hue that resembled gold. "Then those over there." He skipped the central door, which was larger than the others and a translucent grass-green that matched the throne. He pointed at the two on the far side. One of solid black at the end, then then one next to the green door—a twisting swirl of almost every color in the rainbow.

"The ritual happens in that order," Kris said. "My door ..." He walked to the rainbow door. "Is this one, the last one before the Queen."

"Your door?" Erika asked. She had too many questions. She'd only gotten as far as the first door and stood mesmerized by the carved figures of the dragons on its face.

"The doors open to chambers each of the team are fated to enter. I'm not immune to Fate's plan any more than the rest of you. This is my door. That is your door." Kris came back and stood close behind her, his breath audible in her ears. Goosebumps rose up on her skin at the caress of his words. She wanted to spin to face him, kiss him savagely, then fall to the floor and fuck him. She spread her fingers, thinking to reach back and touch him. It was like some strange impulse—another entity—was in her head urging her on.

"You can't touch me," he said in a near whisper that tickled at her skin. "I know you want to, but it isn't allowed. Not by human hands. No one has touched me since I was a child."

"What?" she asked, finally turning to face him and staring at him in disbelief. She tried to remember any moment during their trek when he'd touched another member of her team, but he'd always been oddly distant, camping a little farther away from the rest. She'd interpreted his attitude as a cultural divide of some kind, but his brash declaration by the pool a moment earlier contradicted that.

"I'm destined for this." His dark eyes met hers, intent and steady. He didn't *look* like a crazy man. Should she believe him?

"What the hell is this, Kris? I hope you understand I'm having a very hard time believing what you're telling me. Fated mates, seriously?"

"You and your team are the mates Fate sent to the Court. I'm the sacrifice that will revive all the rest of the brood."

She laughed. "You're crazy. You just need to get laid."

"I'd love to. But you can't help me unless you walk through that door and begin the ritual."

She gave him her best skeptical, scientific once-over. "So how did you get that tattoo? Someone had to touch you to give it to you."

"I've had this since I was a baby."

"You're telling me they gave a newborn baby a tattoo?"

"My mother gave it to me. She was one of them—a dragon—before she died. Two of the monks who helped raise me were also."

"Ohh-kayy ... I believe *that* about as much as I believe you can't be touched." She narrowed her eyes. His story was so outlandish she couldn't wait to prove he was full of shit. The contradicting desires warred inside her. Yes, she wanted this, but she still couldn't believe it was happening.

"I'd love to feel your hands on me, Erika." His voice held a hint of challenge, but she didn't move. She couldn't decide how to start.

"I'll help you out," he said. He stripped off his shirt again and dropped his pants. He stood in front of her, resplendent in his nakedness and glowing in the warm light. Not only did he have the dark coil of the dragon around his sculpted torso, but his strong thighs were tattooed in a scaled pattern all the way up over his hips. His erection was spectacular, too. Long, thick, and uncut, with a glistening bead already dripping from the pink tip that protruded from his foreskin.

Erika reached for him but stopped, her knuckles curling in like she'd hit a barrier just an inch away from him, so close his heat seemed to sear her skin. She shook her head, thinking it was hesitation.

"As much as I want you to touch me, Erika, it can't happen. This magic I'm bound by is too strong. I'm the sacrifice. I'm too sacred for contact, and it's driven me crazy my entire life, but the frustration is nearly over. No matter how hard you try, you can't touch me. Not until we walk through my door over there. Before we get there, you and your friends need to open the other doors. It's my job to watch you carry out the first four stages of the ritual."

"You're telling me you have some magical dragon curse that won't let you come into contact with another human? And what ... that you're destined to be some blood sacrifice to resurrect a mythical race?"

He smiled. "It isn't a curse, and they aren't a myth. I'm a gift to them, and it isn't my blood they want, but my lifetime of pent-up need. You just need to play your part. You've been destined for this. Now that the magic is in you, all you need to do is let it carry you."

"So, we do our part and you get laid? What exactly are we putting on the line here?"

"The Dragon Court's fated mates give up their pleasure, and they awaken."

"Who is this Dragon Court?" she asked.

"They're the ones who make the rules, or they will be soon. The sons and daughters of the previous Court. The rest of the brood sleeps in the other chambers in this place, protected by the Guardians." He reached out and stroked the wing of one of sentinels outside the doorway they stood within. "They're all asleep, but when the ritual is done, they'll be awake. And free to live among humans again. To find mates among your kind. To extend their existence for another generation."

The tattoo around his middle seemed to shift in the flickering light. Kris's cock twitched. Erika slicked her tongue across the smooth inner skin of her lower lip, imagining what he must taste like. She dropped to her knees, intent on proving him wrong, but just knelt poised and fevered at the effort to get closer. Her mind wanted him, but her body was commanded by something beyond her.

"Fuck," she muttered. "Fine, if I can't give it to you, I'll give it to myself."

"Don't," he said, crouching in front of her, but she'd already pulled her shirt open and shoved up her tank top to expose her firm, bare breasts. Her nipples were hard as small pebbles. She pinched them between her thumbs and forefingers—her own favorite brand of foreplay. Twin jolts of pleasure shot straight between her thighs. Having his eyes on her, all smoldering and hungry, just made her hotter.

"Don't what? Don't jerk off in front of you? You like looking at me. I know you do."

"I love looking at you, but this won't help. Your Nirvana is meant for him."

"It'll help me." She unzipped her shorts and shoved her hand down the front. Her pussy was slick, her clit a hard, thick bundle, swollen and throbbing. Erika swept her fingertips over it, sending a rush of tingles through her body. She continued down, sinking into the sodden heat of her channel, gathering wetness, then back up to rub with two fingers over her clit in delicious slow circles. She squeezed one breast in her free hand, rubbing her nipple with her thumb while she watched him. Kris's eyes stayed fixed on the movement of her hand underneath her shorts. After a second, he swallowed and cleared his throat, then met her eyes.

"It won't help."

"It will when I come, and you'll wish you did it to me."

"That's just it. You can't. Your Nirvana belongs to him." He glanced to the tightly closed door beside them.

"We'll see about that." The rush was already beginning, her muscles clenching and her body tingling all over, but it dissipated as quickly as it had begun. She rubbed her clit harder, chasing the sensation she was so ready for—she just needed a little bit more to get there. Her jaw clenched in the effort to find it. She sped up her motions and tweaked her nipple harder, grabbed her other breast and teased, but nothing.

She was *there*! Why couldn't she come? It had never been hard for her to have an orgasm. If she wanted it, all she had to do was this ... exactly what she was doing. Usually it was easier and better if someone happened to be fucking her at the same time, though that had never been a requirement.

"Why aren't you touching yourself?" she asked, breathless and pausing to let her tired muscles rest for a moment.

"I can't." Kris slumped back against the wall and looked down between his thighs at his cock like it was some foreign beast he couldn't quite comprehend.

"What do you mean? You can't touch me and you can't touch yourself either? How do you *bathe*?"

He laughed. "Well, I *can* ... technically, but I learned years ago that it did no good. I can't bring myself off. And you won't be able to ... ah ... *come* ... while you're here."

"Let me guess ... dragon magic." Erika settled back against the wall, too exhausted to keep trying, even though her pussy screamed for release.

He smiled ruefully. "Yes."

"So you've never had an orgasm? That's tragic."

"I have, but only in my sleep. They send me dreams sometimes. It's how I knew you and your team were the ones I was meant to bring. I dreamed of all of you the week before I met you. Especially of you. Probably because you are the leader."

They'd sent him dreams. Had they sent her dreams, too? Were those dreams she'd had her entire life more than mere fabrications of her subconscious mind? More than some secret, erotic wish?

She stared up at the illuminated carving on the door. The polished red and purple colors beckoned to her and she reached out, tracing her finger over the upraised surface of the design. The smooth stone was only slightly cooler under her heated touch, and the colors mesmerized her. Jade came in an array of colors, Eben had said, and was also one of the toughest minerals, nearly impervious to breakage, which the pristine quality of these carvings attested to. It had to have taken years to carve it all; the entire place was decorated entirely in it.

This door included a bas relief image depicting two dragons coiled around what looked like two human figures. It was like looking at a page of the Kama Sutra, the way the angles were just a little off, but it was clear enough for Erika to understand what the image was meant to convey. Two humans, a man and a woman, engaged in passionate coitus with two dragons. Though she had to blink a few times to register the shapes of the dragons. Sometimes they looked like scaled, long-tailed beasts, but if she shifted her eyes the right way, they looked almost human.

"What the hell did you put in our food, anyway?"

"Some spices I cultivated myself known to awaken the senses. Other than that, nothing but the water here. It's been steeping in their magic for hundreds of years. Their need to awaken is very present. This is the time for their ascension."

Kris seemed so earnest, but his need wasn't enough to sell her. She stood up and straightened her shirt.

"I think you're playing us somehow. I have no idea how, but I'll figure it out. Put your fucking pants on." *Before I go nuts.*

As she walked back toward the doorway to the main chamber, she heard behind her, "Erika. You can't leave this place until you've completed the ritual. I didn't trap you into this, but it's the only way to leave."

"Oh? Then why does it feel like I have no other options?" she shot back over her shoulder.

"I'm more than just a guide, so I know it was always your quest to be here. This is where you belong—where we both belong. You know it's true, deep inside. Just translate some of the text and it'll be clear, I promise."

Erika paused for a single step and clenched her fists. If he was playing them all for his own ends, she'd figure it out, but he wasn't lying about her quest. Still, Kris's words were too much fantasy for her to reconcile. She'd found it. That was enough. All she needed to do now was catalog the artifacts and transport the pieces suitable for study and display, then write her dissertation on the entire expedition. After it was published, she would reap the rewards and bask in the professional limelight. End of story.

Except deep inside, she knew there was so much more to the story than that, and more to her dreams. Her father had never been after glory, but his research had led her on this quest, and her dreams had pushed her to complete it. Maybe there was more for her to find besides artifacts. Maybe Kris was the key to uncovering the deeper secrets of this temple. Before she'd walked through those doors at the surface, she would have argued that only science could convince her of the truth. Now she wasn't so sure. With each step farther away from the doorway she'd just left behind, the weaker her hold was on her own convictions until what she wanted had shifted entirely.

She raised her hand up to fondle the small red jade figurine at her throat. It was a childhood dream come true. More than that, it was her life's work realized in spectacular fashion, not to mention her heart's deepest, most secret desire. Her entire body buzzed with the understanding that *this* was what she really wanted. To open that door and find her dragon.

And Erika was used to getting what she wanted.

CHAPTER SIX

Camille's breath finally steadied and she rested her head back against the solid stone behind her. A narrow band of light seeped in from the crack in the doorway leading to the main chamber, illuminating her boot-clad feet where they rested on the stone.

She could still hear Erika's low voice asking questions and Kris's even replies. When she'd followed Erika to the pool, she'd been sure she would catch the two of them screwing, but what she ended up witnessing was so much more interesting. She couldn't quite process it all. She'd stayed far behind and snuck through the open doorway to the rear corridor behind the dais without them noticing, then clung to the shadows, listening to them talk. If she tilted her head forward a tiny bit, she could see them, and ended up rubbernecking while Kris stripped and challenged Erika to touch him.

Camille's mind reeled at all the implications, and she was even more eager to get to translating, but just needed a breather after watching the two of them together. They hadn't even come close to having sex, but she'd never seen such a tense exchange. And when Kris had divulged the secret of the temple, she had to test it herself.

She pictured Eben's broad hand stroking the dragon's penis and moaned softly while she touched herself. The idea that they could all come alive was what thrilled her the most. There had to be hundreds of dragons in here. Most of them were frozen in their native forms, but if what Kris said was true, they could all take the shapes of humans. And according to Kris, the entire team was fated to become the mates of the dragons behind those doors. The thought that one of them might belong to *her* made Camille's blood hum every bit as much as it did whenever Eben looked at her.

Her clit throbbed beneath her touch and the familiar surge of sensation made her speed up to reach that crest. Kris was lying, she thought when she got close to the edge. But just before she climaxed, her pleasure hit a wall. Tension pooled deep in her belly, seeking a release, but nothing was imminent. She groaned out loud and pulled her hand out of her shorts, smacking it against the stone floor beside her. He was right. As much as she wanted it and as close as she was, there was no way she could make herself come. How, though? Their Nirvana belonged to the dragons. What the hell did that mean?

When Camille heard Erika's emphatic arguments echoing toward her, she scurried out the door and back to the throne. At least she knew enough now to know what to look for.

With her penlight and notebook, she crouched down and began translating the characters etched into the base of the dais. After a few hours and a set of sore knees, the truth began to emerge. She made the notes and kept going, forcing herself to exhaustion to avoid the very present issue of how horny she was. Keeping her hands busy was the best means of avoiding what she really wanted to do, and if Kris was being honest, it wouldn't help anyway.

Camille had always admired Erika's easy attitude toward sex and wished she could be that liberated about it. To care so little about what people thought that it made men's tongues fall out of their mouths when she walked by. That's how all the men in their group seemed to behave around Erika anyway. Even Corey, all dark and broody, seemed to *see* Erika for something more than just "the boss." Camille had seen him assess their leader. Maybe not in an overtly sexual way, but the two had talked, and Camille had watched Corey's expressions. She knew he respected Erika and found her attractive in a way that suggested maybe he wouldn't have joined them at all if he didn't.

She shifted her thoughts into the native language while she translated. It was a common ancient dialect, so the act was mindless for her. The pencil was an extension of her brain, transcribing the words as she read them, during which time she could happily daydream about other things. Like Eben doing dirty things to her. His hand stroking that dragon's cock had aroused her incredibly, making her eager for the end of supper when she could have some alone time to pleasure herself while thinking of him. Then all this happened, and now she was practically rubbing her nose on the surface of what was apparently a platform that held the throne of an enigmatic leader of an elusive race. The more she learned, the more she had to keep translating.

The part about the ritual was the most interesting thing. There was one facet of it in particular that drove her out of her mind with desire. They needed a virgin, and as far as she knew, she was the only one besides Kris. No, she was sure of it. She knew Eben and Erika weren't virgins ... they'd been fucking like bunnies most of the trek. Hallie wasn't, Camille knew because Hallie had shared a pregnancy scare story with them one night. Dimitri was the only guy who might've been, but he'd destroyed that illusion after confessing to having shared a girlfriend once with his twin brother. And Corey ... well, you didn't get to be as worldly and experienced as Corey without having sex.

That left her and Kris, and Kris had clearly been destined for a different role in the ritual. And she knew from her personal lack of experience that she was an appropriate subject.

She read and re-read the ritual until it started to sound like a legal document. Most of the ritual components were obvious. They required witnesses, but the virgin component was different. All it said was "... and a virgin's blood to anchor the dragons to the earth." The text very specifically differentiated the "virgin" from the "catalyst," which she understood was the role Kris was meant to fill. He might have been a virgin, but he had no free will, if his own words were any indication. The virgin had to *choose* her mate from among the Guardians at a random point during the ritual. That meant she got to *pick*. She looked up at the pair of huge white jade figures and their enormous cocks and licked her lips.

The gender was very obvious in the language, too. The virgin was intended to be a female. The very visual presence of erect dragon appendages throughout the stronghold made that detail a little less mysterious. It gave her a lot of options, she supposed. She eyed the statue beside the throne Eben had been fondling earlier and stood up abruptly. She walked over to it and crouched down again beside the figure. The dragon sat in a position similar to her own, but with an erect spine, all its weight apparently resting on its hefty tail. Its thighs jutted out parallel to the floor and its wings curled up like twin sails behind it.

She reached out a tentative hand, then paused, looking up into the dragon's eyes. They might be alive. If they were, she couldn't just grab him, could she?

"I'm just going to touch you now," she whispered. "I won't hurt you."

She stretched her hand and gripped the solid column of the dragon's phallus. Her palm hit warm stone and it took her a second to register the incongruity of the sensation. It was stone, and therefore it should've felt cold, but it didn't.

"Oh, you're warm. I wonder what that means."

It meant more research. Camille released him and turned back to the text beneath her feet. Why were they so warm? And why did she have an uncontrollable urge to climb on and fuck one of them?

She rubbed her eyes and wished for coffee, but didn't want to wake the others to make it. She'd just have to power through. The golden shapes of the characters filled her vision when she knelt down again with her notebook and continued transcribing, looking for some enlightenment about the statues and what she'd learned in the corridor. And trying her damnedest not to think about Eben.

CHAPTER SEVEN

"*Geva, what are you doing?*"

Geva mentally smiled at Issa's admonishing tone. He loved pushing her buttons, but more than that, he loved testing the limits of the rules he was bound by.

"*Just trying to keep things interesting,*" he said, pushing another long lungful of red smoke out and sending it into the air of the temple. Breathing was one of the few things their bodies could still do during their centuries-long hibernation, and this was the first time he'd had a reason to use the seductive powers of his smoke in forever.

He could sense them all out there, men and women alike. Three females and four males had arrived earlier that day and had spent several hours exploring. One was clearly the Catalyst, whose particular purpose was to have his dragon nature awakened so he could become the conduit through which they all sent their power to awaken their queen. The others were the mates Fate had chosen to awaken Geva and the rest of the Dragon Court.

Geva wasn't particular about who his magic affected. It was probably cruel of him to use it this way while their pleasure was blocked by the temple's magic, keeping them from reaching orgasm until they began the ritual. But he was tired of waiting, and he was just bored enough after all this time to test the wills of those six humans to find out how far they were willing to go. Could he provoke them into an orgy with each other before they even opened the doors to the Court's chambers?

He was prepared to send another lungful of his breath out into the temple's atmosphere when he heard her voice just on the other side of the heavy door to his chamber. He halted, holding his breath instead, his body tingling from the proximity and the rough, lust-filled sound of her voice. Her need was palpable, and it made his already fully erect cock pulse with all five hundred years of pent-up desire.

"*Erika, please open the door ...*" He made the plea as strongly as he could, hoping it would reach her through their connection.

"*Does your begging mean you finally admit she's real, and that she's fated to be yours?*" Issa asked.

Geva growled. "*I just want her right now. I need her, and you know it. She's perfect for me. Can you hear her? Her hunger is as strong as mine ... stronger ... Sweet Mother, is it possible a female like her actually exists? One woman with a desire strong enough to match my own? If it's true, she'll want what I want. Even if we are perfectly matched, she'll crave the same adventure other playthings provide.*"

Issa let out a dreamy sigh. "*That is the ideal, isn't it? One soul mate to fulfill us, but who understands our needs as well.*"

Geva remained silent, his attention sharply focused on the sounds outside his chamber. He heard her frustrated arguments after she gave up on pleasuring herself. If she would just open the door and find him, he could give her what she wanted. What she needed.

But her voice retreated and the door remained tightly shut.

"No. Come back. Erika!"

With a silent yell of frustration, he expelled another breath filled with his seductive power. This time he infused it with every ounce of his desire for her, hoping it would reach her and bring her back to him soon.

CHAPTER EIGHT

Eben rolled over in his sleeping bag and stared into the darkness filling the cavernous reaches above him. His balls ached and his dick was as hard as it had been when the door on the surface opened, admitting them into the depths of this place. He'd tried sleeping, but his mind kept wandering to images of Camille's full, round ass.

He rolled over and began stroking himself surreptitiously beneath his covers, trying his best to stay quiet. He fisted his cock and nearly groaned out loud in pleasure after the first stroke. He imagined her blonde braid resting along the arch of her spine while she bent on all fours, displaying her perfect ass for him. This shouldn't take long. He'd jerk off, then sleep—his standard procedure during his college days—then maybe dream of Camille talking sweet to him in that melodic, breathy voice of hers.

Except it didn't happen. The ache in his balls just intensified, yet he still couldn't come. He hovered on the edge, but no amount of stroking could bring him past it. Something was very wrong with this scenario. He'd never had trouble jerking off. It had gotten even easier since he'd been screwing

Erika. She was so dirty she'd given him a wealth of material to masturbate to. But his fucking dick was apparently on strike tonight. He couldn't sleep like this. Cold showers weren't an option.

Now all he wanted to do was shove his hot cock into something, and the urge threatened to drive him mad. He threw off his sleeping bag and decided to go exploring to distract himself. There were doorways that they hadn't opened yet. Lots of them. There were the ones behind the throne that he knew Erika was laser focused on. But there were others, too, all locked. Maybe he could find a way to open some of those locked doors and earn a few points with Erika.

Camille's pretty ass waited out there somewhere for him to open, too. He shouldn't go looking for her, but her bedroll was empty, and it seemed the perfect excuse.

He was worried, he told himself. *I wanted to make sure you were okay,* he rehearsed in his head. Not, *I really want to go down on you.* That was an understatement. He wanted to shove his tongue into every single orifice she possessed.

Camille had featured in his fantasies ever since he'd met her when Erika assembled their team. But over the course of the weeks they'd traveled together, he'd become more and more enamored of her—a detail he could never properly articulate to Erika without sounding like a complete pussy. In spite of a generally healthy level of self-confidence around women, he'd been hesitant to approach Camille. Each time he tried, she looked at him like she had earlier that day—like he might just be crazy. He supposed the thing with the dragon cock might have been too much, but damn, she was so beautiful when she blushed like that.

So he kept going back to Erika. Erika wasn't just his oldest friend, she was also the perfect fuck buddy. He wondered if Camille would like having her asshole licked the way Erika did. Fuck, he'd love to do that to her. Even though the mere image of making love to her could satisfy him most nights, for some reason tonight, he couldn't *stop* imagining her in the naughtiest positions. Not just bent over displaying her perfect ass to him, but sometimes doing that with her thighs spread on either side of his face and her pussy poised above his tongue, her sweet mouth wrapped around his cock. Or riding him face-to-face with her full breasts rubbing against his chest.

The vivid image of his dick buried hilt-deep in her ass flashed through his head, making his balls pang almost painfully. Maybe he should just find Erika instead. She might at least be good for a blow job if he promised to return the favor.

Eben got as far as the stone dais and stopped, momentarily dazed by the image before him. Camille lay in the center just before the huge green jade throne, sound asleep. She was on her side, her cheek resting on one arm and her pretty braid draped over her shoulder. Her top had ridden up, and she clenched one breast in her sleep. Her other breast was bare, the fabric of her tank top shoved up above the pink tip of her hard nipple that just begged to be sucked. Christ, he'd do it if he could without feeling like a complete perv. She was too good for him, so pure and naïve and virginal, but with an ass that could halt time. What he wouldn't have given to just once bury his face between those round cheeks and go to town until she screamed his name.

Just a touch, he thought. One touch—she'd never know.

His mouth watered and his cock throbbed when he quietly crouched beside her and reached out. The hard, pink flesh of her exposed nipple beckoned, the areola a perfect pebbled vermilion circle, about the size of a quarter, perched atop the creamy mound of her breast.

"Eben, I need you."

He jerked his hand back like he'd come too close to a flame and shoved it in his pocket, standing with an abrupt turn in the direction of the voice behind him.

"Fuck, Erika. You scared the shit out of me."

Erika glanced at Camille's half-naked sleeping body and eyed him with apparent suspicion.

"You were about to molest Camille, weren't you? You perverted bastard."

"I ... what? No! It's just that ... Fuck, I'm horny as hell, and you pretty much disappeared tonight." It was as likely an excuse as any.

She stepped quietly across the dais and surveyed Camille where she slept. Once by the other woman's side, she bent and carefully tugged Camille's shirt down to cover her breasts, then gently extracted Camille's notebook from beneath the sleeping woman's cheek.

Erika's eyes scanned the pages of penciled scrawl quickly. "Holy shit, he wasn't lying. Eben ... this place is a lot more important than we thought it was." She looked up into his eyes, her pretty face beseeching. "We have to wake them up."

"What the hell are you talking about? Wake who up?"

Erika laid the notebook back down and grabbed his hand. Her dark eyes were wild. She was more excited than he'd ever seen her. With a brief glance he realized how disheveled she was, but it just served to make her sexier. Women like Erika were so good at wearing their fixations like a badge that just made men like him gravitate toward them. Her hair was a tangled mess, her dirty shirt half-undone and wrinkled, her breasts almost spilling out from her low-cut tank top, and her nipples were hard little circles pressing against the fabric.

"Dragons, my dear. They are fucking *real*. That statue you were so crudely fondling earlier? Real. Living, but asleep. I've been walking for the last three hours probably, just trying to figure it all out, but this is the answer. *We* are going to wake them up."

"I think lack of sex has made you a crazy woman."

"Sweetie, I'm just as horny as you are, but apparently that's by design. Kris gave me the scoop. We can't orgasm unless we're touching one of them."

"Ah ... one of what?"

"One of the dragons."

Images of shoving his cock into a stone vagina made Eben crease his brow with worry. "I'm not fucking a rock."

"I don't know how it works with the female dragons, but we'll figure it out. Maybe all they need are facials."

"Right." He laughed. "And the idea of screwing a reptile turns you on? I admit I'm as kinky as the next guy, but bestiality? Not gonna go there."

"They're not *beasts*. They're mythical creatures who actually aren't so mythical after all, and they can look like humans. Kris is one of them. Come on."

"Can't she come too?" he asked, gesturing to Camille. "I'm sure she'd want us to wake her up to see."

"No, honey, this is a two-man job. She's not ready for this, I promise you."

She led him back to their camp, urging him to silence while she found the camera and tripod stashed in Corey's gear.

A moment later they slipped through the now open doors behind the dais and into a shadowed corridor. Kris stood waiting by the first of several recessed doorways, his expression eager. Eben eyed the big, muscular Thai suspiciously, then glanced at the elaborate tattoo that covered his entire torso. If anyone he'd met was more than human, Kris certainly fit the bill.

"Kris, you beautiful man, I changed my mind. Let's do this," Erika said.

Kris nodded and stepped up to the door, placing his hands atop a pair of inlaid characters and reciting a few words in a language Eben didn't recognize. The doors swung open and the room inside blazed to life when all the sconces along its walls lit up simultaneously.

"Wow. This looks like some rich bastard's version of a personal fetish room," Eben said. The first thing he noticed was the wide altar-like platform in the center of the room with the figure of a naked man chained to it—a very aroused naked man, carved entirely out of brilliant red jade. When Eben's eyes traveled past the platform to the end of the room, they nearly popped out of his head.

A purple-hued sculpture of a beautiful woman rested upon a small bench. Large wings stretched out behind her, making her resemble a majestic bird of paradise. The figure was shapely, with plump breasts and a lovely face. And she had huge, swirling horns that emerged from the top of her forehead and angled backward. Behind the horns, her wings stretched out in pure lavender jade so translucent that the lights cast through them, painting the floor like stained glass. Coiling tendrils of hair draped over her shoulders, trailing down to a flat stomach that culminated in spread thighs flanking her bare pussy.

Eben's eyes rested between her thighs, trying to imagine how much fun the sculptor must have had while polishing it to such a brilliant shine. And shine it did, as though she were already wet and ready for fucking. Without even thinking, he gravitated toward her. The shape of her breasts was just about as alluring as Camille's had been. He had no qualms about touching this one, though. When his fingertip grazed the smooth purple stone of her nipple, a bolt of lightning seemed to shoot straight through him. He *needed* to fuck her, but how?

"Eben, aren't they beautiful?"

He turned his feverish eyes to Erika. She'd set the camera and tripod in the doorway and now stood naked beside the prone statute on the platform, wearing nothing but the cord of leather around her throat, from which dangled an ancient jade figurine of a dragon. Her auburn hair had been released from its perpetual ponytail and flowed freely around her shoulders. Her nipples were hard, dusky peaks and her breasts rose and fell with excited breaths. He licked his lips at the glisten of wetness visible between her thighs.

She swept her hand from chest to hips over the contours of the chained man, then slowly up along the rigid shaft of the statue's cock.

"How does he feel?" Eben asked.

"*Amazing.*"

"Let me watch you fuck him." His beautiful dragon woman wasn't going anywhere. From this angle, he could see the taloned feet of the prone man and the hint of scales on his lower legs.

Eben stood and walked around to the head of the platform and stripped off his shirt, then his pants.

"Do it, Erika. Climb on and fuck him."

"Get me ready first?"

"Seriously? You look so lit up right now you're glowing. Touch yourself. I can already see you're wetter than the jungle outside."

She let one hand slide up her stomach and clutch her breast, squeezing her nipple harshly. The fingers of her other hand skimmed through the coarse, roan-colored hair between her thighs and dipped between her lips. Eben's cock twitched in response to the moan that erupted from her mouth when she began stroking herself.

"See, you look pretty ready to me. Give him your best, baby. He's aching for you already, I can tell."

CHAPTER NINE

When Erika looked down at the red jade statue, she still couldn't believe her eyes. The images from her dreams were manifested right in front of her, from his glorious horned head to his strong, clean features, all the way down to the huge, rigid cock that towered at the apex of his thighs. He was huge all over, and her core ached to feel that shaft plunging into her, but she hesitated. Eben was right; she didn't need help readying her body for the dragon's cock, but her mind hadn't quite caught up yet.

Erika glanced at the corner where Kris stood as if he could give her some kind of signal that she was on the right track, but he only stood passive and intent while he watched. It had to be torture for him to witness all this and not be able to find his own release until the end. His lips twitched a bit, which she took as a positive sign.

Returning her gaze to the face of the dragon, a sense of urgency flooded her. It was as though a voice spoke directly inside her mind, even though there were no actual words conveyed. A feeling gripped her—something more potent than her own apprehension. Even though he looked like no more than a lifeless statue, she had the strongest feeling that he *needed* her. That he needed *her*.

She'd never believed in Fate before. She was a scientist, and self-determination was one of her core philosophies—always had been. But in that moment she couldn't shake the powerful belief that her entire life had somehow prepared her for this moment. For this man.

This dragon.

Her dragon.

With shaky hands, Erika climbed onto the platform and straddled the naked statue, positioning herself over the polished jade phallus. Her vaginal muscles clenched painfully, a sure signal that she needed this, but more than that, *he* needed this. Her dragon had been here all along, waiting for her, and it was time for her to give him what he longed for.

She leaned over him, bracing her hands on the solid, smooth mounds of his pectoral muscles, and gazed down at his face. His eyes were closed, the strong, clean beauty of his jaw and chin a contradiction to the almost wicked tilt of the smile that was frozen on his full lips. She smiled back, imagining the lurid thoughts that must have gone through his mind in the moment he was frozen, like he'd been thinking very dirty thoughts.

"He wants you. Can't you see it?" Eben said.

"The feeling is mutual," Erika murmured, entranced by those lips and desperate to find out how they might feel against hers. Her entire body hummed with need when she dipped her head and pressed her mouth to his.

His lips were almost as warm as flesh, and just as smooth, even though they were hard, polished stone. Up close she was startled to discover that his skin had an odd geometric texture. Scales, she realized, though the pattern was small and very faint.

"You're already in love, aren't you?" Eben asked, stepping closer and drifting his fingertips across the red stone of the man's cheek. "I don't blame you. He's ... otherworldly. Are you going to fuck him, or not?"

"Damn, you can be an asshole sometimes. You want to see me fuck this cock, huh?"

"Yeah, baby."

She poised herself over the huge erection that jutted up between the thighs of the statue and pressed down slightly.

"How does it feel?"

"Shut up." She bit her lower lip as the hard tip of his cock parted her slick folds. He was huge ... bigger than any lover she'd had before, and it would take some patience to work herself down onto him.

Eben leaned over the end of the platform and laid his own kiss on the figure's lips.

"You're in love with him, too," she said, breathless at the zing of sensation the silky-smooth stone between her thighs evoked, even with just the tip of it penetrating her.

"I just want to see if he can make you come as hard as I do," Eben said. "Considering he's inanimate. Besides, we never did get to have that three-way and I've always wanted to watch you lose your mind on someone else's cock."

Erika sank down farther, unsure whether she could take the entire length of her dragon's huge jade cock into her, but she pressed harder. Her body buzzed with pleasure when the ridged head pushed past her G-spot and she let out a soft gasp, pausing and enjoying the moment while her channel acclimated to the thickness of him. God, what would it feel like when he had control? A moment later, her backside finally met the statue's hard thighs and his thick tip pressed into her deeper recesses.

"Tell me how it feels," Eben said. He leaned over the end of the platform, his hand clutching at the statue's horns. He gripped his cock in his other hand, clearly wanting to stroke it, but hesitating for reasons she was all too aware of herself.

"Incredible." She couldn't think of any other words. All she knew was that she needed to keep fucking. *He* needed her to keep fucking. Bracing her hands on his chest, she rose up and sank back down with an involuntary moan of pleasure. Fucking him was like nothing she'd ever felt before, and she longed for those eyes to open and meet her gaze—to see how lost she was to the pleasure of simply having him inside her. She kept moving, finding her rhythm, and pumped up and down, each stroke hitting her in just the right places. Every single one ... the shallow little sensitive spot that she could reach herself when she jerked off, and the deeper spots that almost paralyzed her with how good they felt.

Eben continued stroking his cock in front of her. He looked so desperate for an orgasm she felt sorry for him, but within a second, he groaned and his cock erupted in a stream of creamy white semen that covered the statue's face. Erika was on the knife's edge of her own orgasm, and when she watched Eben lose himself, she surrendered. She slammed down on the cock she'd been riding and succumbed to the waves of pleasure. Her pussy clenched on the stone and she cried out, crazed with the exquisite sensation of release. The statue beneath her warmed perceptibly and an answering pulse throbbed between her thighs.

The air vibrated with a loud, guttural sound. Her body shifted up, but she was barely conscious in the aftershocks of her orgasm. She heard the sound of chains breaking, and a moment later, a hard, male chest loomed in front of her. Claws raked her back, making her cry out at the sharp pain that seared her skin, but it was nothing compared to the pleasure still rocketing through her. The cock inside her expanded in girth and a long tongue swept itself across her breasts, leaving her nipples tingling. When she opened her eyes, the shimmering visage of a dragon greeted her briefly before coalescing into the very human-looking face of the man she'd been fucking. Still was fucking. He let out a long, low growl and embraced her, thrusting his cock so deep she grew dizzy.

"I'm awake," he murmured into her ear. "And you ... are *mine*."

He held her close and nuzzled at her breasts. "My Erika. You are a joy to wake up to. So tasty."

She froze, clutching her hands in his mane of red hair. His skin had become the hue and texture of human skin, but his eyes and hair remained the same blood-red as the stone he'd apparently been carved from.

"You're not going to eat me, are you?"

He chuckled and latched onto one of her breasts, sinking his teeth in, but not breaking skin. Steadily, he continued thrusting up into her.

"I might *eat* you, but no ... we don't dine on humans. You're much more fun to make love to." His voice was deep and resonant, the timbre teasing at her eardrums with every word, caressing the depths of her mind as thoroughly as his cock caressed her pussy walls.

"Do you have a name?" she managed to gasp out between panting breaths. She'd come again very soon, now that he was reciprocating.

"I have many names. You awakened me; it's your choice."

"Ah." It was increasingly difficult to focus, but she had to know. "You don't have your own name?"

"I do. My name is Gevaerentethessis. Humans tend to not like long names, though, so you pick one, my love."

"Geva?" she panted.

"Yes, that's one of them. I like it. Your friend is about to die from need."

"My friend?"

"Yes, the one who so graciously ejaculated on my face earlier."

"Oh, god, sorry about that."

Geva licked his lips, but otherwise ignored the splatter of Eben's spend that graced his cheeks. "No need to apologize.

He tastes young and healthy. But very needful. Is he for my mistress?"

"I guess he is," she said, wiping the remnants of Eben's orgasm off Geva's cheeks. "Eben?" She glanced past Geva's shoulder. In spite of an epic orgasm, Eben looked shell-shocked and still aroused.

"Your turn, sweetie." She looked over her shoulder at the purple jade figure on the seat behind them.

Eben walked in a near-dazed state and knelt in between the statue's spread thighs. He always was so attentive that way, Erika thought. He loved going down on women.

"He looks competent," Geva whispered in her ear. The hot breath sent a pleasant tingle down her body that settled right in her clit.

"He is. *Very*."

"Would you like to watch them while I finish my awakening and fuck you?"

Oh, would she. At his urging, she shifted off his lap, regretting the loss of his hard shaft from deep within her, but eager to feel him enter her from behind. She turned and rested on her hands and knees where she could see Eben service the statue of the female dragon.

"I hurt you," Geva said and she felt the sting of his fingertip graze over the edge of the wounds he'd laid into her back when he'd awakened.

"Just a little. I don't mind." She glanced over her shoulder to see a frown on his gorgeous face.

"Let me fix it."

The air shifted around her and he grew in size, red scales erupting over his skin, his head elongating again into the beast she'd only seen for a moment when she climaxed. Geva clasped her naked hips gently in his huge talons as his velvety snout gusted warm clouds of red steam along her back. The sensation made her shiver, but the scratches stung less and less.

"That feels nice," she said.

Geva's forked tongue flicked out from between his jaws, and she shivered as it tickled over her skin. The warm wetness of it slipped around and teased at her breasts, then snaked back and explored between her thighs. Its split tip stroked between her pussy lips, tasting her until she moaned. She stared back over her shoulder at the thick column of flesh that protruded from between his massive, scaled thighs. It was even bigger than it had been when he was a statue, but she craved every inch of it now.

"You like the way I taste?" she asked, and was startled to hear his deep, gravelly, and, despite his bestial form, very intelligible response.

"You taste alive. You taste beautiful. Hmmm, I could taste you for eternity." His heavy claws tightened around her hips, and the way he laid her bare aroused her further.

"Will you fuck me like this?"

"My dragon form is too much for human women."

"Please. I can see you want me. I can take it."

"Oh, I do. I crave filling you with my cock and flooding your womb with my seed. I don't need to be in my true form for that, but if you desire this form, I will go slowly."

The beauty of Geva's dragon form mesmerized Erika even more. His wings stretched out behind him, quivering with the magnitude of his craving to claim her. His glowing red eyes flashed with lust.

He nuzzled her behind and flicked his tongue in a tickling trail along her spine while moving closer. Soon the scorching heat of his thick tip pressed against her entrance.

"Oh, yes! Do it!" she cried out, pushing back, inviting him in deeper.

His rumbling response vibrated through her entire body, amplifying her desire. The stretch of her pussy walls made her groan when he began pushing into her. Her nails dug into the hard stone beneath her and she moaned at the hot, throbbing push of his cock slowly working deeper and deeper.

He let out a soft grunt, pulling back, then pushing in a little more. Then he did it again, pressing farther with each sharp little thrust. Erika's core was spread impossibly wide, and every cell along the surface of her channel felt alive with the contact of his enormous shaft. Slick wetness coated her inner thighs, and she knew it was all her because he hadn't even climaxed yet. Good god, and she'd asked him to fuck her like this, when the man hadn't had sex in how long? Centuries, based on the data she'd gathered about this place.

But the intensity of Geva's need mattered little once he was fully encompassed within her. He paused and let out a long, low growl of appreciation, his talons digging into her hips only a little harder.

"So tight, but your sweet cunt took all of me. You *were* made for me, weren't you, Erika? Fate chose well."

He bent his long head down over her shoulder, teasing his tongue over her breasts again. He moved carefully at first, fucking her with long, languid strokes, filling her up while she watched Eben attentively lick the female dragon's jade pussy.

"Worship her pussy well and you will be rewarded," Geva said to him. "You can fuck her to life that way."

The words made no sense to Erika, as full as she was with Geva's cock, but Eben apparently understood and licked with increased fervor. He groaned in elation a few moments later, then rose up on his knees. Eben looked like he was about to fuck the statue, though all Erika could see was his tight, muscular backside and the clench of it when he thrust into the statue like she was actually real.

Through her fevered haze of ecstasy she asked, "Geva, what did he just do?"

"He woke her up. That part of her, anyway. The rest will come. Now that I have you wrapped around my shaft, I need to feel your Nirvana again. Need to fill you with my seed, and then mark you, sweet Erika."

All it took was the rumble of his deep voice and a series of solid thrusts that reached the deepest parts of her. His heat and solid, urgent thrusts sent her spinning. She was already halfway there when she felt a caress between her thighs and very human-textured fingers found her aching clit and began to rub in tight little circles.

Erika let out a long moan at the rapture flooding her. Her eyes fluttered closed and her body spasmed, rocking her in an earth-shattering orgasm. Geva roared above her, giving up to his need and slamming his massive cock in deep one last time. A second later, his semen filled her, the pulsing jets heating her core and adding to her ecstasy.

CHAPTER TEN

Geva held Erika's hips tight against him for a few ragged breaths before he slowly receded, his entire shape dwindling to human again and he pulled her with him. He fell backward against the warm stone and held against his chest in his strong embrace, his panting breaths still gusting warmly against her ear. She rolled over, looking into his red eyes.

"I just fucked a dragon, didn't I?"

Geva chuckled and cupped her cheek. "Yes. And you will again, because you and I are fated to be together. You are mine, Erika."

His smoldering gaze softened, his expression flooding with wonder. The revelation in his eyes mirrored a feeling that had been growing in her soul since the first climax on his glorious cock.

"What is it?" she asked softly.

His lashes lowered and he pursed his lips together. "You'll think me mad."

"I doubt what you have to say can be any crazier than the day I've already had. You didn't exist in my world until tonight. And now ... Now I can't imagine a world without you."

Geva lifted his gaze, eyes flashing, and the pure emotion there penetrated her defenses until her heart fluttered with the strangest feeling of how utterly *right* this was.

"I never believed it was possible, to find a female so perfect, so deliciously carnal. Fate can be so cruel to my kind, but I see I was wrong to doubt Fate's intentions. Here you are. The perfect mate. A reason for love I never thought I would find."

Erika's stomach flipped and tears pricked her eyes at his use of the word "love." It was so unlike her to get emotional with a guy, especially one she'd fucked only moments after meeting him. But here she was, so moved by his words she ached to feel him inside her again in a way that would let her illustrate the intimacy she felt between them.

"It *is* mad, isn't it?" she said, smiling up at him through half-shed tears. "That you've been in my head most of my adult life, and I feel like I already know you. Because I think I do, Geva. I know you. I've known you for a long time, and I know I already love you. And trust me, those aren't words I just throw around. Neither is 'fate.'"

"Sweet Erika, I love you, too," he said, and pressed his mouth to hers, hungrily pulling her into a desperate kiss that did everything and more to reflect his words.

A moment later, she was able to catch her breath and she became aware of other sounds echoing through the room.

She glanced down to the bench where the other dragon had been and let out a giddy laugh.

"Oh, Eben. Why does that not surprise me?"

"She seems to like him," Geva said.

Eben was now seated on the bench with a pretty violet-haired woman riding him. After a few minutes, the purple-haired beauty yelled out a resonant cry and her wings unfurled, then embraced them both in a violet cocoon. Erika could just barely hear Eben's familiar orgasmic yell as his hands clutched at the dragon-woman's bottom, yanking her down hard on his cock while he came.

"Who is she to you?" she asked, glancing up at Geva.

"My friend, then my keeper, of a sort. I misbehaved before hibernation and had to serve out the sleep bound in chains as punishment. Issa was assigned to ensure I stayed put until the hibernation spell was in place. My penance has been done, now that you have awoken me."

"So what happens next?"

"Now, we make love some more. Every climax we share feeds the Queen's well. Soon we awaken the twins. And I do hope you brought a virgin with you. She's the secret ingredient. The magic will tell her what to do all on its own."

"A virgin?" Erika asked, but became distracted when he shifted down her torso and his tongue elongated and slipped between her thighs. He toyed with her clit until she couldn't think straight, swirling the forked tips around and around, then dipping the agile length into her tender depths and finding her sensitive inner flesh. Erika gasped, her hips bucking reflexively up to meet his mouth. He gripped the backs of her thighs with both hands, spreading her wider for him to devour, which he did with far more enthusiasm and skill than any lover she'd ever had. For some strange reason, she had the sense that he really *was* a starving man, hungry for the taste of her orgasm.

And, oh god, was she more than willing to let him have every last drop he wanted to take from her. His tongue retreated from her channel and his lips wrapped around her clit, suckling it while his tongue worked her to her climax yet again. He let out a hungry growl just as she got close, then hoisted her hips up tighter to his mouth at the exact moment she lost control and her orgasm overtook her.

Erika grabbed his head, tangling fingers in Geva's hair as she cried out his name, her voice echoing hoarsely through the chamber. He slowly relaxed, continuing to tease her gently as she came down from yet another spectacular climax. Her breathing gradually returned to normal and she glanced down at him where he remained propped on his elbows between her legs.

He seemed to be studying her pelvis with interest, and before she could ask what was so fascinating about her bush, his tongue lashed out in a series of stinging strokes right over her womb, above the dark brush of curls that covered her mound.

"Ow, what was that?" she asked, alarmed, but still fascinated by the spark of power behind his eyes.

"You are mine, my love. This mark is our bond."

She stared down at the glowing red shape that had appeared on her skin. With it came an overwhelming certainty that her life was complete in that moment.

"Where do I get to leave *my* mark on you?" she asked.

Geva gave her a lazy smile. "Your mark was burned into my heart the moment you woke me, my love." Then he slipped his tongue out again and swiped the forked length of it up along her soaked slit once more, his lids lowering as though he were savoring a tasty treat.

"How do you do that?" she asked when coherent thought returned to her.

"I can transform any of my body parts at will into the shape I desire. My natural form is this ..." He sat back on his haunches in front of her while his body shimmered, and a second later he was a huge, resplendent red dragon, four times the size of a man. Then his tail disappeared and his legs became human, along with his torso. All that was left was the dragon head atop the very beautiful muscular shape of a man with a massive hard-on.

"Show me your human face again. I like that face."

He smiled at her when the face reappeared. "I like this face, too. But my human tongue is not as functional as my dragon tongue."

"No, your dragon tongue is definitely much more ... ah ... functional."

"I thought you'd prefer that one," he said, grinning at her with perfect white teeth. God, he was pretty. He even had dimples. But what amazed her the most was how perfectly he embodied the creature she'd seen in her dreams for so long, not only visually, but in every sense. He truly was the perfect man for her, though the awareness of that simple fact made her remember the friend who'd shared this particular quest with her the longest. The friend who had also been her lover for years, but who had never quite measured up to her dreams, despite his qualities as a man.

She glanced at Eben and saw him in a tender conversation with the dragon-woman, who was now curled up on his lap, nuzzling at his cheek. The woman really did like him. Her wings were still extended and drifted through the air in a lazy rhythm, sending pleasant gusts across Erika's skin.

"I want to make you come again." Erika heard the words while watching Eben mouth the very same ones to the dragon girl on his lap. It took her a second to realize that the words she'd actually heard had come from Geva, not Eben. She extracted herself from her fascination with Eben's tryst to pay attention to the far more fascinating creature in front of her. Her own dragon.

"I could make love to you all night, but I have work to do," she said. "We need to awaken the twins. How do we do that?"

"If the guide has followed the laws of the ritual, you will have brought enough humans to complete all the phases."

"Yes, there are seven of us, counting Kris."

"Their mates will call to them when the time comes. We just need to keep making love until the next phase begins on its own, so you choose. Work, or ... um ... *work?*"

"Kris can't just go lay hands on the doors and make them open like he did with this one?"

"Kris has a very specific role to fill here," Geva said. His glance into the shadowed corner reminded her that they'd had an audience all along.

Kris nodded. "I can only open the first door. The others will open when each phase is due to begin, but it won't take long."

"How does making love to you help open the doors, anyway?" she asked Geva. She climbed onto his lap and slipped his erection inside her again, sighing with the sensation of fullness that ensued.

"Every door has a key, my love." With that, he thrust deep, pulling her into a languid kiss that left Erika no doubt she had found the dragon of her dreams.

About Ophelia Bell

Ophelia Bell loves a good bad-boy and especially strong women in her stories. Women who aren't apologetic about enjoying sex and bad boys who don't mind being with a woman who's in charge, at least on the surface, because pretty much anything goes in the bedroom.

Ophelia grew up on a rural farm in North Carolina and now lives in Los Angeles with her own tattooed bad-boy husband and four attention-whoring cats.

You can contact her at any of the following locations:
Website: http://opheliabell.com/
Facebook: https://www.facebook.com/OpheliaDragons
Twitter: @OpheliaDragons
Goodreads: https://www.goodreads.com/OpheliaBell

Printed in Great Britain
by Amazon